THE SECRET COVE

Gwen McCutcheon
Art by Mike Rooth

GRAPHIC READERS

Literacy Consultants
David Booth • Larry Swartz

Ru'bicon www.rubiconpublishing.com

Editorial Director: Amy Land
Project Editor: Dawna McKinnon
Editor: Jessica Rose
Creative Director: Jennifer Drew
Art Director: Rebecca Buchanan

Printed in Singapore

ISBN: 978-1-77058-563-8
3 4 5 6 7 8 9 10 11 12 2016 25 24 23 22 21 20 19 18 17 16
4500568937

What **happens** when a new marina **threatens** the gentle **manatees?**

CHARACTERS

Mandy

Grandpa

Dakota

Tala

Each summer, Dakota and Tala spend a month at their grandpa's house on the beach.

One day, they attend the opening of a new marina.

I am happy to say that the new marina is now OPEN!

Grandpa is not happy about the new marina.

The marina is nice to look at, but it isn't good for all the wildlife. It will bring more boats and more pollution to our community.

While Grandpa prepares lunch, Dakota and Tala go exploring.

Let's go that way!

It also says they are gentle creatures.

That's the sea monster we're afraid of?

The next morning, Dakota and Tala try to spot the manatee again.

Do you see it?

There she is! She really *does* look friendly!

Dakota and Tala visit Mandy every day. One day, they notice something different about her.

The next day, Mandy is still acting strange.

I think she's hurt!

Let's get Grandpa. He'll know what to do.

Dakota and Tala tell their grandpa about Mandy.

Will she be OK?

I don't know. I think Mandy may have been hit by a boat.

She probably swam here to recover after being hit. The new marina has brought many boats to the area.

With their grandpa's help, Dakota and Tala make signs asking boaters to slow down.

11

All too soon, it is time for Dakota and Tala to leave.

We'll come back next year, Mandy.

I'm going to miss this place — and Mandy, too!

Comprehension Strategies:
Asking Questions
Summarizing

? ? ? ? ?

beginning   middle   end

Common Core Reading Standards

Foundational Skills

3c. Decode regularly spelled two-syllable words with long vowels.

4a. Read on-level text with purpose and understanding.

Literature

1. Ask and answer such questions as *who, what, where, when, why,* and *how* to demonstrate understanding.

3. Describe how characters in a story respond to major events and challenges.

5. Describe the overall structure of a story

Reading Foundations

Word Study: Antonyms

High-Frequency Words: beautiful, boat, book, city, each, happy, house, idea, moves, much, really, summer, time, water

Reading Vocabulary: area, boaters, cove, creatures, grandpa, manatee, marina, monster, secret, signs

Fluency: Reading in Phrases

BEFORE Reading

Prereading Strategy   Making Connections

- Introduce the book by showing the cover to the group. Read the title aloud.
- Turn to page 2. Say: *Let's make a text-to-world connection. Can you make a connection between manatees and other animals that are threatened?*

Introduce the Comprehension Strategy

- Point to the Asking Questions and **Summarizing** visuals on the inside front cover. Say: *Today we are going to practice asking questions and summarizing. We ask questions to be sure we understand what we read. Summarizing means using your own words to retell only the most important ideas and events in a book. Asking ourselves questions as we read will help us make a summary at the end of the book. There are 6 question words: who, what, when, where, why, how.*
- Point to the question at the top of page 2 and read it aloud.

   Modeling Example Say: *This question lets me know that the manatees are in trouble. It also brings other questions mind. Why are the manatees in trouble? When will they be safe? Where will they stay until then? Who will save the manatees? How can the manatees be saved?* Draw a large hand on the board and write the five *W* questions on the fingers and *how* on the palm. Say: *We will use the answers to create a summary.*

- Say: *Good readers summarize because it helps us understand what a story is about. We ask questions as we read to make sure we understand the events.*